The Legend of Sleepy Hollow

RETOLD AND ILLUSTRATED BY

WILL MOSES

FROM THE ORIGINAL STORY BY

WASHINGTON IRVING

PHILOMEL BOOKS ～ NEW YORK

For my wife, Sharon,

and my sons, Jerry and Lloyd

—W. M.

Copyright © 1995 by Will Moses. Published by Philomel Books,

a division of The Putnam & Grosset Group, 200 Madison Avenue, New York, NY 10016.

Published simultaneously in Canada. Printed in Hong Kong by South China Printing Co. (1988) Ltd.

Book design by Gunta Alexander. The text is set in Sabon.

Library of Congress Cataloging-in-Publication Data

Moses, Will. The legend of Sleepy Hollow / Washington Irving; retold and illustrated by Will Moses.

p. cm. Summary: A superstitious schoolmaster, in love with a wealthy farmer's daughter, has

a terrifying encounter with a headless horseman. [1. Ghosts—Fiction. 2. New York (State)—Fiction.]

I. Irving, Washington, 1783-1859. II. Title. PZ7.M8477Le 1995 [Fic]—dc20 93-21910 CIP AC

ISBN 0-399-22687-7

1 3 5 7 9 10 8 6 4 2

First Impression

AUTHOR'S NOTE

We Moses have a long tradition of storytelling in our family. Some have chosen the spoken word, while others, namely my great-grandmother, Grandma Moses, my grandfather, Forrest K. Moses, and now me, have chosen to tell our stories through paintings. Living here, nestled among the villages, farms, and rolling hills in the eastern reaches of the upper Hudson Valley, where the Cambridge and Hoosick valleys merge, many of these painterly stories seem to be just outside our window.

Grandma Moses, whom I only knew when I was a child, started painting back in the 1930s. Times were hard on the farms then, and she took up painting as a means of bringing in a little extra money. Her paintings were so wonderful, always telling a story. Grandma's son, Forrest, who was my grandfather, also painted and taught me most of what I know on the subject. He too realized, as do I, that our paintings must tell a tale. Gramp always told me, "Each painting should be a story in itself, one that little girls and boys can understand, but also one their mothers and fathers will appreciate and love."

Long ago, Washington Irving, a neighbor of ours (if you count the length of the Hudson Valley) wove his story, telling magic with words. He left us with a rich heritage of remarkable tales of the 18th century Hudson Valley. Most famous of these is *The Legend of Sleepy Hollow*, long revered as an American classic.

In this retelling, I wanted to accomplish two things. I wanted Washington Irving's basic story to be told with a feeling that was true to the original, but also in a way that might make it better appreciated and understood by young people today. Secondly, I wanted my paintings to reflect and enhance this great tale in the mind's eye of young readers and listeners. I have two young sons, and this story is really for them.

This is the approach I took with this book, writing and illustrating as if it were for my own children. I hope I have succeeded in meeting the expectations of these most honest and important critics. I also hope that I have told and illustrated *The Legend of Sleepy Hollow* in a way that Washington Irving himself would have liked.

THIS STORY all happened down in the lower Hudson Valley of New York State, not so far from where I grew up, way back when America was still a very young country.

Nestled near the banks of the Hudson river, and populated by folks of Dutch and German blood, lies a mysterious, dreamy little settlement called Sleepy Hollow.

Since time before time, there have been stories among the settlers in the Hollow of evil deeds from the past that still hold a power over the valley and the people who live there. Some say a high German doctor bewitched the area in early days. Others claim the evil deed was done by a long-dead Indian chief, maybe a prophet or a wizard.

Whether Sleepy Hollow is indeed bewitched, I don't know for sure, but I think it must have been. The folks who lived there were certainly given to believing. Tales of ghosts, haunted spots, and twilight visions were plentiful. Reports of strange voices and music floating on the night air were so common that no one really thought of them as unusual.

King of the tales and spirits who haunted the valley in those days was a ghostly, headless figure riding on horseback, said to be the ghost of a Hessian soldier, whose head was shot off at the shoulders by a cannonball during the Revolutionary War. Most folks believed that he was searching for his missing head while on his midnight rides. More often than not, he did travel the roads near the church-yard where the body of this unlucky soldier was buried.

One thing is certain—the old churchyard was an eerie place, with night winds blowing and howling, probably caused by the rushing headless horseman himself, racing back to his grave before the break of day. That's what I believe!

Now one day, a schoolteacher by the name of Ichabod Crane wandered into this strange, dreamy land. Traveling from his home in Connecticut, and seeing the need for a school, Ichabod Crane appointed himself the new schoolmaster and started a school for the children of Sleepy Hollow.

The name of Crane was perfect for this fellow Ichabod, for he was very tall and lanky, with narrow shoulders, and long, gangly arms that far outgrew the sleeves of his clothes. He had a small flat head that was decorated with big ears; his eyes were large, glassy, and green, and his nose was misshapen, looking much like a hawk's beak. At a distance, I thought he looked a lot like a scarecrow.

Ichabod Crane's school-
house was a ramshackled
affair. It only had one room,
and the windows, many
broken, were pasted and patched

with pages from old schoolbooks. The door always seemed to swing
with the breeze, as the only way to fasten it was with a crooked stick
and twine. But Crane at least picked a nice spot for his schoolhouse.
It was situated at the foot of a hill, near a bubbling brook with a
handsome birch tree in the yard.

The broken-down schoolhouse may not have been picture-
perfect, but the purpose of Ichabod Crane's school was education.
And educated is what his students would be! Those who failed to
learn quickly and properly could count on the sting of Ichabod's
birch switch across their shins. I don't want you to think he was
cruel to his students though. No, he handed out his brand of justice
with fair measure. The weak and
timid were spared the worst,
while the stubborn and
wrong-headed could
expect a double dose.
When school was
over, Ichabod easily
became a playmate and

chum for some of the older children, and when the weather was bad or the day was dark, he would shepherd the younger children home to the safety of their families. I should say, however, that the children who had pretty older sisters, or whose mothers were especially noted for their cooking, seemed to be given this special attention far more frequently than others.

Now, you know, back in those days the schoolmaster was paid very little for his services, but part of his pay was room and board in the homes of his students. Each family would take a turn, for a week at a time, providing Ichabod with a bed in their home and giving him his meals. The old Dutch farmers generally liked Ichabod. He would make himself welcome by helping out around the farms, mending fences, splitting wood, or helping with the haying.

The Dutch wives of Sleepy Hollow were also fond of Ichabod. He could be charming, and he helped around the homes, feeding chickens, churning butter, rocking the cradle; or showing special attention to the younger children. He had one other quality which endeared him to the old Dutch wives. This was his appetite! Ichabod simply could not be filled, and the Lord knows he would try. The Dutch farm wives prided themselves on their cooking and considered feeding the skinny, gangly Ichabod a special mission of mercy.

Oddly enough, Ichabod was also famous throughout the valley for his singing ability. He was the undisputed singing master of the Hollow church. On Sundays he would lead his band of chosen singers through the morning's list of psalms in a spectacular fashion. Schoolmaster Crane was even able to make a few extra and badly needed coins by giving singing lessons to some of the local folk.

All in all, Ichabod had made quite a satisfactory life for himself in Sleepy Hollow. His needs were comfortably taken care of and, because of his respected position as schoolmaster as well as his singing ability, he was in fact admired by many of the young ladies in the region. He carried on courtships with an elegance and grace to which his rival country bumpkins could not dare to compare.

The truth is, though, the schoolmaster was an odd mix. He was intelligent and popular, yet he would delight for hours in the tales of mysterious happenings that were told about Sleepy Hollow. The more tales he heard the more he wanted. No story was too monstrous or unbelievable for Ichabod. Often after school he would lie down on a lush clover bed near the school, reading and re-reading the witching tales of Cotton Mather's *History of New England Witchcraft*.

Then as the evening dew fell, Ichabod would sulk homeward into the twilight with his imagination racing, inflamed by the very sounds of the surrounding countryside. The moan of the whippoorwill and the cry of the frogs would make him uneasy, and the rustling cattle or hooting owl would send him into full fright.

When poor Ichabod was spooked this way, he would sing his psalms at the top of his voice, hoping to drown out the noises of the night and fend off any lurking spirits. In the winter when his clover bed was covered in frost and snow, he would listen to the old Dutch wives as they sat spinning wool, telling ghastly tales of ghosts and goblins, haunted fields, haunted houses, and particularly the tale of the headless Hessian horseman that haunted Sleepy Hollow. But when the evening came to an end, Ichabod Crane would always

find himself in the familiar predicament—a long and frightening walk through the dark of night back to his home of the week.

Despite all the terrors and frights of the Hollow, our schoolmaster friend continued getting along quite nicely there, until one day his path was crossed by a force more powerful than even Cotton Mather's witchcraft!

It was a beautiful young woman by the name of Katrina Van Tassel, one of Ichabod's singing students, and the only daughter of a wealthy Dutch farmer, named Baltus Van Tassel. Katrina was a blooming fresh girl of eighteen, plump and rosy-cheeked. Ichabod Crane easily fell in love with her, attracted by her intelligence, her charm, and her radiant beauty.

These qualities alone would have been reason enough for most men to love her, but Ichabod was cast from a different mold than most men. The day of his first visit to Katrina Van Tassel, Ichabod was overwhelmed by the sight of her father's farm. It was nestled on rich bottom land bordering a nook of the Hudson river, and was a vision of prosperity. His glassy green eyes surveyed lush fields — planted full with wheat, rye, buckwheat, and Indian corn — orchards of fruit, and lush meadows where fat cattle and sheep were contentedly grazing.

Shaded by a mighty elm tree, the farmyard itself was alive with activity. An impressive spring of water bubbled near the enormous tree. Nearby was a splendid main barn surrounded by several smaller farm buildings, all bursting with activity. Pigeons and martins adorned the roofs and swooped through the air. In the pig house, Ichabod could see magnificent porkers with their little suckling pigs.

In the farm pond there was a gaggle of snowy geese, and a flotilla of ducks; back in the yard, large-breasted turkeys were on a patrol, searching for the occasional morsel, and close by, ranged chickens and guinea fowl, watched over by a magnificent rooster. Before him lay what seemed to be unimagined prosperity and a lifetime supply of wonderful suppers. If Ichabod Crane ever doubted his desire for Katrina, that doubt was certainly gone now.

Ichabod couldn't waste time and couldn't make a mistake in his courtship of Katrina Van Tassel, because as you might have expected, Katrina did have other suitors. The most formidable among them was a strapping lad named Brom Bones. Brom Bones was the hero of the county, famous for his handsome looks, feats of strength, horsemanship, and his eagerness to frolic and fight. I knew him best, though, for his famous pranks and jokes, from which no resident in the Hollow was spared.

Bones and his band of followers would often be heard at all hours of the day or night riding hard, whooping their war cries, having just won a wager or pulled a new prank. At the end of the day though,

Brom Bones was just another lad without direction in his life, with one exception. That exception was his desire and love for Katrina Van Tassel. There were plenty of rumors that, while she thought him something of a brute, she was not altogether sorry to see him riding down her farm lane on summery Sunday afternoons. Bones's interest in Katrina persuaded most other men to keep their distance. As fetching as she was, most men did not think her worth the thrashing Brom Bones would certainly give them if he found them out.

Ichabod Crane, however, was not most men. After figuring all the risks and the rewards, he happily rose to the challenge. Ichabod devised a plan calling for him to make his advances to Katrina when visiting at the Van Tassel home to coach the wonderful Katrina in voice and song. Evening after evening the schoolmaster and the

Dutch beauty would warble together under the giant elm in the evening twilight, with the spring bubbling gently nearby. A romantic setting if ever there was one! Even Ichabod couldn't have imagined things going so well.

Days passed and Ichabod's plan was not obvious to most folks in the Hollow, but it was soon clear enough to Brom Bones. Bones was furious and boasted he'd double Ichabod up and lay him on a shelf in his own schoolhouse. But Ichabod heard the boast and made certain never even to give Brom the chance.

Not to be discouraged though, Brom Bones and his band of men commenced pestering Ichabod with endless pranks; they smoked out his singing class at the school by stopping up the chimney.

They broke into the school at night and turned it topsy-turvy so many times that Crane thought witches were meeting there. When the schoolmaster passed by, Bones would call him names and poke fun at him. He even taught a stray dog to whine in a most unpleasant manner, then introduced the dog around the Hollow as Ichabod Crane's singing master.

This sort of nonsense went on until one sultry autumn afternoon a messenger riding a wild pony arrived at Ichabod's schoolhouse. The schoolmaster was in a frazzled state of mind. The endless pranks and insults had taken their toll.

The messenger entered the school and presented Ichabod with an invitation to attend a festive evening of merry-making at the Van Tassel home that very evening. You may be sure the schoolmaster's spirits quickly rose. The students were hurried through their lessons and were dismissed from school an hour early.

Ichabod groomed himself to perfection to present his best appearance at Katrina's home later that evening. He borrowed a horse, such as he was, from Hans Van Ripper, the Dutchman with whom he was staying that week. Surly and broken down, with a rusty, burr-infested mane and tail, the old plough horse had seen his best days long ago. Still, while one eye was blind and glaring, the other eye had the fire of the devil himself in it! I suppose, if you can judge by his name—"Gunpowder"—in his day he must have been quite a horse.

Ichabod mounted the beast with all the dignity and pride of a knight from old. In reality, though, his appearance was quite different. Ichabod rode with short stirrups, long legs and knees drawn high up, his bony elbows sticking out at the sides, looking for all the world like a giant grasshopper.

Even so, as I said, the day was a fine one, and as he made his way to the Van Tassel home, Ichabod thoroughly enjoyed the sights. The late afternoon sky had a crimson and yellow glow, and the autumn harvest was bountiful. Ripe apples hung heavy in the trees, and fields of golden yellow corn were everywhere. Squash and pumpkins were being picked for winter, and wasn't the air filled with birds and bees taking advantage of the wonderful weather. The sights and smells made Ichabod's mind race with visions of wonderful apple pies, squash pies, and corn cakes spread with honey by Katrina's delicate hand.

His mind was steadied and fortified by these sweet thoughts, as he and Gunpowder plodded toward the Van Tassel farm that day. As he approached, he found the yard alive with other merry-makers. There were the old leather-skinned Dutch farmers and their stout wives and round-faced children all decked out in their best velvet clothing, buttons and buckles, shiny and bright.

The center of attention, however, arriving with a thunder and roar, was the hero of the territory himself: Brom Bones, riding his trusty, but nasty horse, Daredevil. Daredevil and Bones made a good team, as both were full of mischief and spunk. I heard it said that Bones would only have animals that others considered vicious, that an animal full of tricks and treachery was the only kind suited to a man of his good spirit.

When Ichabod entered Van Tassel's parlor, he ignored the bevy of admiring young ladies and did not stop to stare at the silver and pewter that bedecked the room. His first thought was not even of Katrina. Instead, Ichabod made a beeline for that banquet table.

There spread before him, like all of King Solomon's gold, were platters of cakes, trays of doughy doughnuts, crumbling crullers, sweet cakes, ginger cakes, honey cakes, and the whole family of cakes. There were pies: apple pies, peach pies, and pumpkin pies. Mingled in this horn of plenty were hams and smoked beef, preserves of plums, peaches and pears, broiled shad and roasted chickens, bowls of milk and cream and a giant teapot sending a rapturous vapor of sweet steam all around this higgledy-piggledy mix of delectables.

Quickly and efficiently, Ichabod assembled a mountain of cakes, meats, pies and fixings on his oversized plate and made for a corner of the room where he commenced to devour every morsel. You could see his spirits soar with each forkful, and his eyes roll with each swallow. Ichabod was in his glory, chuckling and chortling away as he imagined that he might one day be the lord of all this luxury and splendor. Oh how quickly, he thought, he would turn his back on the old run-down school and how he would snap his fingers in the face of any sour old Dutch farmer.

Jolly, plump Baltus Van Tassel was mingling among his guests, offering each a handshake and dose of good humor, when the echo of music was suddenly heard throughout the house. A fiddler had begun to play and the sounds of music rustled the dreamy schoolmaster from his fantasies. Ichabod Crane prided himself on his dancing talents nearly as much as on his singing ability.

When he frolicked onto the dance floor, not a limb nor fiber was still; to see his loosely hung body in full motion, clattering and clanking about the room, you would have thought St. Vitus, the patron saint of dance, was cavorting before you. During this entire spectacle, his dance partner was none other than Katrina, who all evening seemed to be taking the utmost delight and enjoyment in all of the schoolmaster's advances.

Meanwhile, Brom Bones sat watching—brooding jealously over in a corner of the room.

After the dancing ended, Ichabod joined with some of the farmers who had gathered to smoke their pipes and tell war stories. Quickly, though, as often was the case, the stories turned into ghost and goblin tales. Now, as I said before, Sleepy Hollow is a strange and dreamy place, and so there was no shortage of wild tales to tell. There were stories of funeral trains, reports of shrieking cries in the dark near the great tree where the hapless Major André was hanged. Tales of the woman in white who haunts the dark glen at Raven Rock, screaming her death cry on winter nights.

But soon enough they got around to the tales of their favorite, the Headless Horseman! Much was said, you may be sure, about how the ghost rider had been active lately, especially in the vicinity of

the old churchyard where the Hessian
is buried. Then old farmer Brouwer
leaned forward into the circle of men.
Speaking in a whisper, he told how he
himself met the Hessian in the dead
of night, apparently returning from a
haunt up in the Hollow.

He told of how the Headless Horseman
rode up and forced him onto his horse, then chased him full gallop
over road and field, until they came to the old plank bridge spanning
the stream not far from the church.

The area near the bridge—spooky even on a summer day—was,
in the dark of night, most frightful! Old Brouwer feared for his skin.
Then all at once, the headless Hessian rider changed into a skeleton,
tossed Old Brouwer into the brook, then sprang away over the
treetops in a flash and clap of thunder.

An uneasy quiet came over the storytellers, who had by then drawn into an ever tighter circle, when Brom Bones leaned forward and began to speak. One evening, while returning from a neighboring village, Brom said, he encountered the night rider.

He challenged the headless fellow and his goblin horse to a race—for a bowl of punch—and claimed that he would have drunk the victory punch, too, as he and his horse, Daredevil, easily trounced the ghost. But as they came to the plank bridge, the Hessian bolted and disappeared in a flash of sparks and fire!

None of this was lost on Ichabod. Still, he took his turn to speak, reciting some of his old anecdotes from his book of New England witchcraft. But here is what I think: all of this just frightened him all the more.

Slowly the party began to break up, as the night grew late. The merry-makers loaded up their wagons and carriages and rattled home, but convinced he was on the high road to success in the arena of love, Ichabod lingered for a while to court Katrina.

What was said or what happened between these two would-be lovers late that night, I don't know, but something went terribly wrong, for when he sallied forth, he went not dancing, but crestfallen.

It was the witching time of night when Ichabod, discouraged and defeated in love, mounted old Gunpowder and started his ride homeward. The night was as dismal as Ichabod himself. His only company was the melancholy chirp of a cricket or a sad hoot of an owl. And now as Ichabod rode into the dark, those stories of ghosts and goblins began creeping into his mind. Never had he felt so alone. What was worse, he was approaching one of the spots long famous in ghostly tales: coming up, hard ahead, was the giant gnarled tulip tree where Major André had been hanged at the hands of British soldiers.

As Ichabod approached the gnarled and twisted tree, he commenced a nervous whistle. As if to answer him back, a whisper of wind whined through the dead tulip tree leaves, drowning him out. When he came closer to the tree, he thought he could see something pale and hanging in among the limbs. Ichabod looked closely, hoping that what he saw must be a missing patch of bark, blown away from the tree trunk by a lightning strike.

Suddenly, he heard the loud, lonesome groan of large limbs rubbing, one against the other. His teeth started to chatter and his knees began knocking against the saddle. Ichabod and Gunpowder gingerly rode by.

But not far ahead, there was a small brook that ran into a marsh and thicket, called Wiley's Swamp. There was an old log bridge crossing the brook and the entire area was covered by a tangle of wild vines

hanging from the oak trees. There was faint moonlight filtering through the vines, reflecting a delicate fog rising off the water. Seeing this sight, Ichabod imagined this bridge certain to be haunted by ghosts and witches of the most unspeakable kind!

Calling up all of his courage, he went forward into the fog, his heart thumping like a great parade drum. He hoped to dash quickly across and gave Gunpowder a barrage of kicks to the ribs, but instead of charging forward the obstinate old horse lurched sideways into a fence. Ichabod gave the old beast another series of jabs to the sides, only to have him plunge to the opposite side of the road and into a twisted nest of brambles.

Now, the schoolmaster spared no mercy on the old horse, giving him another round of heel kicks and a lash from his whip. Gunpowder jumped forward, snuffling and snorting as he went. Suddenly though, he stopped, nearly sending Ichabod headfirst into the murky waters below.

Just then the rustle and thump of a horse's pawing hoof caught the attention of Ichabod's sensitive ears. Not far off in a grove of trees, Ichabod could see something huge and misshapen—something black and towering—seemingly ready to spring upon the unsuspecting traveler. Ichabod's hair rose straight on end and his toenails curled under with terror. After all, what could he do? To race away was useless; what chance could he have against such a horrific goblin?

"W-wh-oo arrre you?" he finally shouted out.

There was no answer. So he shouted again. "Who are you?"

Still no answer.

Ichabod gently gave Gunpowder a nudge in the sides, said a prayer, and started to sing a psalm tune. As Ichabod and Gunpowder trotted over the bridge, the specter in the woods rode up along Gunpowder's blind side. Even though the night was dark and dismal, Ichabod could tell it was some form of monster, certainly a horseman of huge proportions, mounted on a powerful black horse. The horseman did not say anything or even threaten Ichabod, but just continued to jog along beside Gunpowder.

Ichabod's mind was racing with the tales of Brom Bones and farmer Brouwer of the galloping Hessian. He thought perhaps if he sped up, he could leave his midnight companion behind, but when he did, the ghost rider quickened his pace as well. Then Ichabod pulled up, hoping the goblin would continue on, but the dark horse and rider stopped, too. Ichabod's heart sank in despair; he tried singing again, but this time his mouth was so dry from fright that he could not utter a sound.

The riders continued their eerie journey down the lane until they crested a small rise in the road, where to Ichabod's terror he saw his companion rider silhouetted against the open night sky. Ichabod was horror struck—he could clearly see now that the giant rider was headless! His horror only grew when he saw that the rider carried what appeared to be his head on the pommel of his saddle.

Ichabod delivered a series of kicks and blows to Gunpowder. He prayed to give the goblin ghost rider the slip with his fast jump. Away Gunpowder and Ichabod dashed—stones and sparks flying with each bound. The specter, however, started right in after him.

Soon enough though, they came to a divide in the road which turns off to Sleepy Hollow. Gunpowder was running like a young stallion, seemingly possessed by a demon himself. Ichabod wasn't in control of his horse, so the old beast went the wrong way and leapt headlong down the lane to the left. They were racing straight for the Sleepy Hollow bridge and cemetery.

Gunpowder's panic had given Ichabod the edge so far in the chase, but as they were halfway to the plank bridge the straps of his saddle broke. Ichabod nearly fell to the road below, but somehow managed to grab the old horse about the neck and mane. The schoolmaster was jostled fiercely about on the bare bony back of the old horse, but the sight up ahead cheered him. He could see the plank bridge, church, and cemetery reflecting in the lunar glow. This was the very spot where Brom Bones claimed the specter disappeared. If he only could reach the bridge, he too would be safe. Another kick to Gunpowder's ribs, and the old horse thundered onto the wooden bridge. When Ichabod reached the other side, he turned to look, expecting to see the specter vanish in a hail of sparks, fire and lightning.

But to his shock and repulsion, he saw the goblin rise in his stirrups and throw the severed head straight at him!

Ichabod tried to avoid colliding with the horrid object, but it was too late; it hit him hard—with a tremendous crash. Ichabod tumbled headlong into the roadway below as Gunpowder, the giant black steed, and headless rider raced past him like the wind.

The next morning Gunpowder was found, minus his saddle and munching a breakfast of autumn grasses at the farm gate of his owner Hans Van Ripper. Ichabod did not show up at school at the appointed hour, and as he had not been seen at breakfast that morning either, an alarm was raised and a search begun. Later that morning searchers came upon Gunpowder's saddle trampled in the dirt. From there the trail of hoof prints that deeply scuffed the road surface were followed to the plank bridge. On the opposite bank they found Ichabod's hat, and splattered around the mysterious scene were the remains of a shattered pumpkin! The deep waters of the nearby stream were

searched in an attempt to find the schoolmaster, but all to no use. Ichabod Crane had disappeared.

The following Sunday a group of church-goers gathered at the spot where Ichabod's hat and the pumpkin were found. Remembering the frightful stories recently shared by Farmer Brouwer and Brom Bones, they figured that Ichabod Crane must have been carried off to his doom by the headless Hessian himself. The schoolmaster's belongings, including his book of New England witchcraft, and a book of Ichabod's feeble attempts at love poetry for Katrina, were gathered and burned. As Ichabod was a bachelor, had no family and owed nothing to anyone, no one in the Hollow bothered to give the missing schoolmaster another thought.

I would be remiss, though, not to tell you that several years later an old farmer on business in New York claimed to have encountered Ichabod Crane. He said that Crane was now a judge in the ten-pound court and claimed that he left Sleepy Hollow for fear of the headless ghost goblin and a broken heart. Brom Bones I always suspected of knowing more about the eventful night than he would ever admit to, for shortly afterwards he married Katrina and always had a twinkle in his eye when the story of the schoolmaster was told.

As for what really happened to Ichabod Crane, you will have to decide for yourself. I, however, agree with the old Dutch housewives who firmly believe he was spirited away by the fearful headless Hessian horseman. The old Dutch wives are, after all, the best judges in matters such as these.

THE END

WASHINGTON IRVING (1783–1859) was an author and diplomat well known for his essays, stories and satirical pieces. Born in New York City, Irving began his literary career by writing about New York society and the theater. After an unsuccessful attempt to save a branch of his family's hardware store in 1815, Irving began writing full-time. His stories "Rip Van Winkle" and "The Legend of Sleepy Hollow," published in 1820, made him world-famous as a writer. Among other works, Irving wrote several essays on his travels through Europe and the United States, and a five-volume biography of George Washington.

WILL MOSES began painting at the age of four with his grandfather, Forrest K. Moses, a folk painter who himself had learned to paint from Anna Mary Robertson Moses, the legendary Grandma Moses. As a fourth-generation member of this renowned artistic family, Will Moses has always felt free to experiment with paint. He has had several acclaimed gallery shows in the United States and Canada, and has toured Japan, where his art is eagerly collected. Mr. Moses' paintings can be found in the collections of the White House, the Smithsonian Institution and the New York State Museum.

Mr. Moses maintains the Mount Nebo Gallery & Farm in Eagle Bridge, New York, which produces and distributes his original graphic art. He lives there with his wife, Sharon, and their two sons, Jerry and Lloyd.